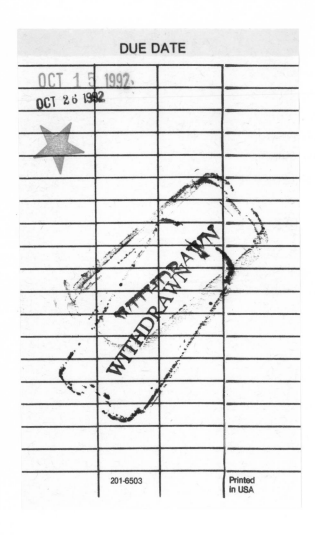

DUE DATE

A decent, sensitive, intelligent but quite uneducated peasant boy, Tomás, grows up accepting without question all he hears about the Jews of the Ghetto, believing them the foredoomed property of the Devil. He also accepts the harshness of the feudal system under which the lord owns not only the land and its wealth but his people as well. Although he shares in the general adoration of the handsome, gay, charming, but heartless young lord of the manor, he is delivered over to an old Jew of the Ghetto to be his bond servant. The Jew has a sweet young granddaughter to whom the lord is strongly attracted. Because she rejects him the young nobleman is party to a terrible revenge.

How Tomás responds to all this, the important part he plays, and the change wrought in his thinking by his daily life among the Jews are the essence of the story.

A
BOY OF OLD PRAGUE

A
BOY OF OLD PRAGUE

S. ISH-KISHOR

drawings by
BEN SHAHN

Pantheon Books

Library of Congress catalog card number: 63–15482

To Frances and Ariane Ruskin

The endpapers of this book are reproduced from a sixteenth century map of the city of Prague.

A
BOY OF OLD PRAGUE

I am a peasant and the son of peasants; my name is Tomás, and I was born in the year 1540 on the domains of a great Bohemian lord, near the city of Prague.

With my father and mother I worked in the fields of this lord four days a week, and on our own bit of land the other three days. Our soil was hard; the crops were poor, for we could not afford to let the land lie fallow when it gave out. Our food was black bread and turnips, and we thrived on it when we had enough to go around; only some years we scarcely saw bread, but only turnips, and rotted ones at that.

One year everything went so well that we even had meat—yes, we had meat four times that year. The tax collector nearly found out that we were cooking meat, because somehow we let a little smoke get through the hole in our roof. But a neighbor ran up and warned us, and we quickly buried the pot of meat and Father stuffed some damp straw into the fire, so that when the tax collector's man came up we could tell him it was the straw that smoldered. So we escaped being taxed on the meat. Next day we told the story to some other villagers, but they never let the secret out. Even my little brothers for once held their tongues.

As soon as the dawn came up over the fields we set out to work, splashing through the dew in the golden sunrise. The tree trunks were a wet throbbing black, but their upper branches were drowned in gold. Mother walked before us, with little Greta on her bent back, pulling at her hair. Mother had long, thick hair. The neighbors said she had been pretty when she was a girl, but I only

remember her with hollow cheeks and heavy large eyes, very clear. Now I think of it, I wonder I did not carry Greta myself, big boy that I was, but Mother never asked me to, and I suppose boys don't think of those things themselves. When it rained, we left the baby with old Fanka, the village nurse-woman, while we went to our work.

One day there was a great storm, and Mother, who was afraid of thunder and lightning, felt sure that some evil was going to happen to us. She trembled, and her hand went up to her eyes every time the lightning came. When we got home at night, shivering and drenched, my little brother complained that he felt ill. Mother looked around at him, her face twitching, and burst out weeping, with loud, hysterical sobs that frightened us.

She made Wenzel lie down; she petted him, and put what few coverings we had over him; she took off her garment and put it on him, and from me too she took part of my clothes. But Wenzel still shivered, and Mother lay down by him and held him in her arms to keep him warm.

Next day, the chief stableman called me

from the fields to help him clean the stalls. I found an old piece of horse blanket among the straw, and took it home at night to cover Wenzel. It did not seem like stealing, the blanket was such an old, holey, ill-smelling thing; but I got a good whipping for it when the stableman found out.

A few months after Wenzel died our young lord Rainier rode home from court. We were expecting him any day now, and there was much stir and excitement in the castle; everything was scoured and cleaned and freshened, hangings were aired, floors were strewn with fresh rushes, the stone walls were scrubbed—the very air smelled washed. Everybody put on his best clothes, or at least cleaned his old ones, and the housekeeper gave new ribbons to the maids.

I was helping temporarily at the castle, for the work was enormous. In the afternoon we saw a great bustle down in the courtyard. People stood around the walls three or four deep, cheering and waving away. My lord rode in at the very head of the cavalcade, splendid in his black velvet cloak and blue satin doublet slashed with silver. His French page, who had fallen behind, was just galloping across the drawbridge when my lord began to dismount without help. I don't know why I took it into my head to do the page's task, but I ran forward and held his stirrup.

He looked down at me with curiosity, as if I were a strange insect, as he swung off his black horse. Just then his page came running breathlessly up, raising his hand to hit me, but my lord, turning, snapped his fingers and cried, "To heel, Lucien!" (Hunting terms were always nearest to his tongue.)

Monsieur Lucien tossed his head and frowned, but he let me alone, and followed my lord up the stone steps. I fancied my lord had called him in, in order to save me from receiving a blow. I did not know, then, the hard and careless heart he had; there was place in it only for his dogs and his horses, and a little for Monsieur Lucien, whom he favored for possessing the same qualities as his animals—high blood, nervous temper, and jealous devotion.

A few days later I heard that my lord Rainier had said I should work in the stables instead of in the fields. I was very glad, for

now I could lord it over all the other boys. And besides the honor of working at the castle, one had always enough to eat there, and covering in cold weather and a stone roof instead of a mud or thatch one full of holes. I thought my lord had really noticed me, and I boasted of it to the boys when I saw them. Lord Rainier seemed to me the handsomest, most gallant and noble gentleman in the world; I even thought that he did not see or understand how his serfs lived, and that was why he continued to tax them so heavily and work them so mercilessly. I thought of a hundred ways of giving my life for him—as boys do think of their heroes—but he never appeared to need it, so I continued to hold my life in trust for him, as it were.

My lord soon returned to the Emperor's court at Vienna, and it was nearly a year before he came back again. He was in high spirits this time, for he had betrothed himself to a great lady, the daughter of a duke; it was an excellent match, and besides, the lady was beautiful and loved him. So there was even more excitement this year when he came, for he was going to give a great banquet to the gentlemen and ladies of his estates.

We were very busy at the castle, but I managed to get away for an hour to go down to the village and see my family and the boys and girls. My cheeks had grown plumper and redder; I had always been called "Plumcheeks," for the rest of the family were thinner and paler by nature. My hair was rather long, too long for a peasant, and my father warned me that I might get into trouble some day because of it, but the girls teased me, and said I was proud of my smooth black hair and wanted to be taken for a person of good birth. I don't think that was true, but I did like to look well, and as nobody seemed to mind, I kept on wearing it as long as the pages wore theirs—down to just below my ears.

My mother was not well, and I gave her a few cakes which one of the maids had gotten for me. I had to watch her, to see that she ate them herself instead of giving them to my greedy little brothers and baby sister.

I walked back along the edge of a thicket, so as not to trample on the new-sown fields.

A light wind, smelling of fresh earth and green forests, was blowing delightfully. I was trudging on, whistling, and breaking the twigs under my feet, when I heard a rustling too strong for the winds to make. It came from a pitlike cleft in the earth, which was filled with clumps of thorn. By now, I heard moans, too, and as I listened they changed to gasping barks and tired whining. I understood that a dog must have been caught among the thorns, and perhaps lay there hurt and unable to move.

The sharp spines of the thorns looked so threatening that I half made up my mind to go away. But first, I looked down into the shallow pit. Holding onto the stumps and roots with one hand, I took each branch separately with the other, and pushed them away from me as I climbed down. The thin, almost invisible long spines filled the air with prickles, and I had a good many scratches on my hands and neck before I had clambered down the few yards of slope. I was nearly thrown over by a long gray body that leaped at me, howling. It was my lord's favorite

hound, Bichette, with a large thorn in her foot.

My eyes swam dizzily and my breast throbbed with fear. If anyone should find me with the lost dog, it might be thought I had stolen her, and that would mean a short rope and a long death without any doubt. I turned to get away, but the dog barked threateningly, and followed me on three legs, with a begging look in her brown eyes, holding out her wounded paw to me for help. So I sat down in despair, took the beast's foot on my knee, and did my best to extract the thorn gently.

The poor thing howled with pain, but she was a thoroughbred, the best in Bohemia, and she let me pull it out. When it was over, I petted and stroked her for her bravery, and she licked the wound. I tore off a piece of my shirt, and bound up the foot as well as I could, and then I helped the animal out of the thorns. I started for the castle again, and Bichette followed me limping, with bent head, as if ashamed of herself; now and again she turned with a savage movement and licked my hand.

I never expected the enthusiastic reception

we got at the castle! My lord's dogs always came into the dining hall at meat-times; he had missed Bichette and had found out that she was lost. His rage was frantic; he declared that whoever had stolen her should die on the rack, and he had already had five peasants flogged on suspicion. He swore and stormed for an hour, and finally sat down to dinner in such gloomy wrath that the servants hardly dared come near enough to set the dishes on the table, and even Monsieur Lucien preferred to keep his distance.

A wild shout arose as I came into the courtyard with Bichette; a dozen servants flew ahead with the great news. I was dragged into the dining hall with the dog. Bichette leaped at her master with deafening barks, putting her paws up on his shoulders and licking his face madly.

My lord gave a cry, and hugged the dog in his arms, shaking her to and fro. His rage fell off him like a cloak, and he was as cheerful as a lark. When he saw the wounded foot, tied up with a bit of shirt, his face grew serious; he took off the bandage himself, flung it away, and shook his head as he examined the wound. Then he ordered the dog to be taken away and properly cared for. Yes, he did love his animals.

When my lord noticed me, standing foolishly in the middle of the hall, he asked me if it was I who had found the dog. I stammered, "Yes," for I was still afraid. But he smiled and gave me his hand to kiss; and I drew my first free breath since I had found the dog.

"Why," he exclaimed, after asking me where I had found her and what had been the matter with her foot, "why, the boy's no fool! I have half a mind to make him my page. He resembles Lucien a little, and they would make a pretty pair!"

Now of course, my lord had no such intention in this world, for I was a peasant and a serf, while Monsieur Lucien was a gentleman of birth no lower than my lord's own. But my lord was a great tease when he was happy. He laughed heartily at the expression on Monsieur Lucien's face. If it is not impertinent to say so, we did look a little alike, for he also had black hair and a rosy complexion, but his skin was much fairer, and his features and limbs were smaller and more delicately shaped.

"My lord—you say I look like—like that peasant rogue?" he exclaimed, his tongue tripping with vexation.

"By my faith, you do," laughed my lord. Without a moment's hesitation Monsieur Lucien drew his little sword and flew at me. I threw up my arm, so that the flat of the blade came down heavily across my wrist.

"Lucien! Enough!" cried my lord, but he was laughing so much that it was mere luck that his voice was intelligible at all. Lucien turned away, breathing hard and sulking, and I hung my head and felt very miserable, for I knew I had an enemy now.

My lord sent me away, and I went down to the kitchens to get my dinner. But this matter had made me too late for it, and I had to go without. For several days my wrist hurt so much that I could hardly do any work with that arm. Then I was told that I must work in the kitchens now, instead of in the stables, for Monsieur Lucien had declared that he thought I had caused the accident to happen to the dog, so as to save it and get into favor with my lord. I don't think my lord believed this, or I would have been severely punished for such a crime; but he let Lucien have his way, and I went with a heavy heart into my new work. For taking care of horses and dogs is men's work, but kitchen work is for maids, and is all indoor work, and dirty and greasy besides. I was also ordered to cut my hair short — another attention from Monsieur Lucien.

My lord was married that year—in 1556, I think it was—and gave so many banquets and balls that the castle was in a continual state of bustle. Never in my life had I seen so many ladies and gentlemen; it seemed there were always stately nobles with swords jutting out under their cloaks, and pretty ladies in long velvet robes descending from their pillions at the great entrance gates. That was not an unhappy year, after all; I often had the opportunity to go down to the village for a few hours. But what we boys liked best was to steal away and go down into Prague, especially at fairtimes.

We used to save a few pennies to buy gingerbread and beer, but when we got to

town and saw all the pretty young girls going by and laughing, it usually ended in our buying gay ribbons and sugar-sticks for them. Sometimes we walked across the bridge and right up to the gates of the Ghetto, and saw there old wrinkled Jews hobbling about the gloomy streets. They looked so dark and melancholy and strange, in their horned hats and long robes, that we boys threw stones at them through the open gates, and bet each other that we would hit someone three times out of five.

Once Ludvic—he was one of the kitchenboys, too—had a bad fright. He was a poor shot and seemed unable to hit anyone at all. At last he got so angry, what with the jeering and mockery of the other boys, that he took up a large stone, aimed it very slowly and carefully, and hit an old Jew right on the forehead so that he bled. Everybody congratulated him and slapped him on the shoulder, and he stood there looking around and grinning, and we watched to see the old Jew hobble quickly off.

But instead, he began walking toward us. We were rather scared, especially Ludvic, for

we thought the old fellow would cast a dreadful spell over us. We would all have liked to run away, but we would have felt ashamed, afterwards, so we kept still. He reached us at last; he had black hair and brows, and those black earlocks, and a long beard, half-gray. His face was dirty and wrinkled, and a slow red stream wriggled down his forehead and caught in his bushy eyebrow.

When he came near, he looked at us with such a mournful, soft expression, that Ludvic plucked up courage, and began shouting, "Here comes the Christ-killer! Here he comes! Yoo-oo!"

The Jew stopped within a little distance of Ludvic and said, very quietly:

"My boy, I pray that you may live long enough to have drawn from you blood as old as mine." Then he turned and walked slowly off, dabbing at his forehead with his hand.

We looked at each other, quite puzzled. Ludvic was red as fire; his lip stuck out, and he breathed fast.

"Do you think that was a curse, Tomás?" he whined. "I'll wager the old fellow cursed me! Why, these Jews can live a thousand years by their magic, and then the Devil gets their souls for it! Do you think that's what he meant, Tomás?"

"I don't know," I answered. "If he did, it's worse luck for other people than for you!" So we all laughed, and Ludvic said he was sorry he hadn't pulled the old fellow's earlocks; and he said he would have done it, too, in a minute, if he had waited. But we jeered him, for he was the worst coward imaginable. So he kept quiet.

Just then a girl came running by, within the Ghetto gates. She was tall and rosy, and she was laughing and looking back at a little boy whom she led by the hand. He could hardly keep up with her; his fair hair was flying, his little breast was lifting up and down very quickly, his eyes blinked, and he could not catch his breath for laughing. It made me shudder; they seemed so natural, yet they were Jews and accursed and the Devil must have their black souls when they died. We began to feel scared, and when Nikolas moved off we went after him gladly. We met some of the kitchenmaids soon after and quickly forgot what had happened.

I did not have time to go to our hut that day, although I had bought a little gift of spice cake for Mother, so I had to give it instead to Margreta. She was a pale, fat girl, not pretty, but so good-natured and full of fun that we could hardly have done our work without her in the kitchen. She would talk to the pans and the dishes while she was drying them, as if they were persons, so that we could hardly stand for laughing. The poor girl was madly in love with my lord's valet; he liked her very much and would have married her, but when they went to ask my lord's permission, he told her roughly that she was too ugly to marry anybody, and that he would not let tall Auguste waste himself on her. Poor creature! She hardly said a word to us that day, and dried the pans so meekly, in such a frightened sort of way, that we were worried and tried to comfort her.

"Don't grieve, Greta," I said to her, just to cheer her up, but feeling so sorry that I might have meant it. "If you'll wait for me, I'll marry you."

She turned on me in a fury. "I don't want you!" she shrieked, and dashed out of the kitchen, howling, her dishtowel still under her arm. I was rather angry with her for her rudeness, but I forgot all that soon, for next day she was found in the river.

But that was after the time I am talking about. Then she was still with us, and as gay and jolly as a host of those foolish traveling jesters that came and made bad jokes and wanted the best of the kitchen in return for them. She used to save the most appetizing bits for Auguste, the big glutton; he came regularly after every meal to make fun of her and get the good things. But he really liked her, and after her death he was so glum and dull that my lord sent him away.

On the day I was speaking about, Greta scolded me for not having gone to my mother, and at first she would not take the piece of cake, but it looked so fine, all gilded, and shaped like a pig, that she took it at last, and I believe Auguste got it. She told me to let her know when I was going home, and she would give me something good to take with me.

But I did not manage to go home for a long while, it was so busy at the castle. One afternoon as we were preparing the food for a banquet to which a great many people were coming, I saw someone loitering outside the kitchen door. I went out to see who it was. It was my father.

Fearing that he might be noticed by the servants or guards in the courtyard, I pulled him in with me. I was vexed at his coming, for I had planned to go home the very next day, and now it would seem as if I was going only because he had reminded me, and as if I did not care about seeing them.

"I wish you could have chosen another time to come," I muttered. Then I was sorry, seeing how pale and hollow-cheeked he was and catching sight of my own healthy cheeks in the back of a frying pan that hung on the wall. So I added:

"I am coming home tomorrow for a little while, but you see I could not get away today."

My father looked at me sadly.

"Sickness does not wait," he said.

"Who—who is it?" I stammered, quickly imagining one after the other of my brothers lying ill. But I knew it was Mother.

"Is she very ill?"

He nodded. I remembered Wenzel; my head went hot and my heart went cold. How could I possibly get away to see her?

"It isn't only that she wants to see you, Tomás, but—but—" His voice trembled into an almost soundless whisper. He drew me out of the doorway, and I felt his lips at my very ear. Food? Steal food from my lord's kitchens? Horror made me breathless. Did my father want me to be hanged?

"But she will die," he said.

"I'll try to," I stammered, to be rid of him, and he went off. As soon as he had gone, I realized that I would have to try, and to succeed.

That night I suggested to the chief stableman that I should go into the courtyard and help to have the guests' horses stabled. He agreed gladly, for he knew he could depend on me, and he was anxious to get to his own dinner. So I did not have to serve at the kitchen door, which would have kept me busy and spied upon all night.

It was raining, and the horses had to be covered and led very carefully over the slippery stones of the courtyard, for the straw we scattered on the ground was soon soaked and useless. There was only one torch to see by, and it too was so blown upon and rained upon that not one of the gentlemen refrained from cursing as I or one of the other boys helped him to dismount. At last they were all arrived, and the rest of the stableboys vanished; but I said I would remain, in case there were late-comers.

I stayed at the door, one eye on the court-yard and one on the kitchen. When, for a moment, the kitchen was left empty, I darted in, and snatched a plump chicken, all hot and dripping with gravy, from a great dish where a couple of dozen of them were steaming, ready to be taken in. I stuffed it into my opened doublet, and turned my back just in time, as the maids came in to bring the dish to the doorboys. I ran for the door and dashed out breathless.

The torch was flickering now black, now red, on the wet stones, and I could not control my eagerness and my fear; I foolishly began to run. Before I had gone ten steps, a huge black mass reared up in front of me, kicking and moving strangely; I felt a sharp bang on the leg and fell down. I had stumbled into a horse and rider.

In a fierce temper the rider stooped down, cursing and beating me with his whip. I did not dare to attract more attention by rising, so I lay still on the cobblestones, hoping that he would pass on when his rage had cooled. But he must have thought I had fainted, or was killed; he called out to some footmen who had run toward him:

"Pick up this rascal, and see if he is alive."

Alas, I would have thanked him if he had had no pity on a peasant, and had passed on. But when I heard him speak, my strength all died in me. It was my lord himself! How did he happen to be there when we thought he was in the castle?

The servants picked me up, half-dizzy with the fall and with the blows. My lord peered down in the flickering thin light of the torch.

"What is he holding?" he questioned.

It was the chicken that I was carrying, pressed to my breast, forgetting my danger in the instinctive desire to keep it safe. The servants tore it away from me and held it up by the legs. My lord's lips loosened in a smile of amazement.

"The young thief," he said calmly. "Hang him at noon, tomorrow, publicly, for an example. Have the guests all arrived and has my lady found her emerald buckle?"

"Yes, my lord, yes, 'twas in the other jewel box," answered one of the footmen eagerly.

"Very well." My lord clicked his tongue to the horse, and then suddenly drew rein again. He looked down at me with a queer expression.

"Hark ye, Girard," he said at last to one of the footmen, "I've changed my mind. Take him to—you know—the house where I have just been. I had to promise the old devil a servant."

By now Monsieur Lucien had run up, and I saw by the light of the torch that he was looking at my lord with such a strange sort of mixed expression: hurt, reproachful, angry— not quite, though, but I'd never seen anyone look at Lord Rainier that way. Nor had I ever seen my lord turn his face sharply aside like that, almost as if he had lost pride.

As he helped my lord dismount, Monsieur Lucien exclaimed, as if he couldn't help it, "Surely it's some witchcraft that takes you there—"

"It may be so," my lord replied, as he walked on into the castle, with his hand on Lucien's shoulder, while someone led his horse to the stables.

Yes, he answered without anger, but there was something in his voice that turned me cold, as though he were only pretending to be calm about whatever had happened.

I was too deeply relieved by his decision not to hang me to worry about what his vague-sounding orders might mean. I let Girard and Paul bind my hands behind me and lead me off through the castle grounds, down the hill, toward the town. They said nothing to me except to tell me to walk faster. They were cross at being obliged to make this journey before dinner.

The town gates were locked, but the guards opened them at Girard's demand. We marched through muddy streets so wet and uneven that I nearly crippled my foot stepping into a hole; Paul swore and took hold of my arm, for, being bound, I could not balance myself. We walked and walked, and I grew desperately hungry; hardly anyone was out in the rain, and the lights of the inns which we passed looked like the very lights of heaven. At last we came to a desolate open space, where the old bridge crossed the dried-up moat. My mind refused to admit where we were! Before us loomed the high walls and triple gate of the Ghetto!

My heart gave a leap of terror and I stopped still.

"Come on, Tomás," grunted Girard, not without a trace of pity in his voice. But I actually could not move for horror. I knew now what my fate was: I was to be bond servant to a Jew!

I had heard rumors that my lord occasionally sold one of his peasants to a Jew, although this was against the law both of the Emperor and of the Pope. But who would complain against a powerful lord in favor of a serf? The Emperor would never hear of it, and if he did, he would certainly not trouble himself over a serf sold, or murdered, or given to the Devil!

I held back heavy as a dummy, while Paul and Girard pushed and dragged me to the gate. They whistled three times, and the watchman came slowly out of his cottage beside the wall. He was a Christian, and I thought he looked at me with a mocking wink. As we passed through those terrible gates into the abode of the accursed, I remembered all the dreadful tales of witchcraft and black magic I had heard told of the Jews. One night came back to me, when we boys had sat together over the kitchen fire, eating nuts and apples and telling terrible stories about the Jews: a Jew had cut himself up in pieces, and put himself into a flask, and had become immortal; another had made himself invisible with the herb Andromeda when the Devil came for his soul; another had turned the sun red with the stone called heliotrope, and another had cut off his shadow and given it to his master the Devil in a cave; another had brought on a terrible storm by means of a copper basin. I thought I saw the Archdemon himself grinning over the walls; I made one prayer to the Virgin Mary, and fainted.

The next thing I remember was Paul's

awed whisper: "See, he came to as soon as I made the sign of the cross over him!"

I sat up, shaking out of my hair and eyes the bucketful of water they had half drowned me with. Paul's rough lips were puffed out with pity.

"Look here," he said, "I'll give you this, Tomás. My mother gave it to me, and probably I'll begin having my fits again if I give it away, but I'll give it to you because, by the blessed Mary, you're worse off than I am now." As he took from his neck a black ribbon with a little silver cross on it, and hung it around my neck, I could have hugged him for gratitude. The watchman gave a short, stiff laugh, swung his keys, and said:

"Be quick with your business, boys!"

The tall, gloomy houses were solid black and terrifying in the night; their gabled tops seemed to waver and mock at me, and here and there a lighted window stared like the eye of a devil. I wondered weakly how anyone could have the cruelty to do what my lord was doing to a Christian soul.

At last we came through the muddy streets, as crooked and close as an eagle's claws, to a high, narrow house, bolted and dark. A black cat gliding between my legs nearly upset my balance again, so weak was I with terror. The men made me lean against the wall while they knocked with rapid, impatient blows at the solid wooden door. The whole street resounded with the noise they made, and I heard its ghostly echoes reverberating through the house, as if no human beings lived inside.

Finally, slow, shuffling footsteps were faintly heard within; a small square of wavering light appeared in the middle of the door, and a cautious voice said, some time after:

"Who's there?"

"Let us in, you old devil-skinner," responded Girard promptly. "You know where we come from."

A long process of unbolting, unbarring, and turning of key after key presently resulted in the door being opened halfway. Girard pushed his way in, Paul took hold of me and led me sympathetically into the narrow hallway, that smelled damp and stony as a grave.

Behind a lighted taper I saw the sharp, dried-up face of an old man, his eyes screwed up into nothing, his scraggy beard making

his head look even more pointed. I muttered a prayer as he looked at me.

"Here's the boy my lord has promised you," scowled Girard. "Mind you don't cut his heart out and bake it for Satan's supper."

The Jew shrugged his thin shoulders in the gray gaberdine, on which the yellow Jew's-wheel stood out like a blasphemy.

"Remember and take it off the account," Girard grunted. Paul muttered, "Goodbye, Tomás," and the next minute I was alone in the bleak hall with the Jew and the lighted taper. Girard and Paul were gone, and I heard their footsteps as they ran in the rain.

What could I do but follow the old creature as he went muttering before me? We climbed up a crooked staircase cut out of the stone, where I could see the green moss on the wall and thought every moment to slip and break my neck.

The old Jew pushed open a door into a large, warm room. There was an Eastern carpet on the floor, and several couches around the walls. A fire roared in the grate. The Jew left me alone for a while, and I crept nearer the fire, and looked around the room.

There was a low table, from which the

chairs had been hastily pushed back; on it was a board painted with red and black squares, with funny little wooden figures tumbling out of a box beside it. These, I thought, must be puppets which the Jews had made, in order to prick them and cause the death of the Christians whom they represented. On the floor, face upward, lay a painted rag doll.

I looked up, and nearly fell backward into the fire. The Jew was approaching me with a large knife in his hand! Now I knew why I had been bought! It would soon be the Passover festival, when the Jews kill Christians in order to drink their blood! My scalp pricked, my blood felt thick and dry, my heart beat loud and fast, and I saw nothing for a moment.

The Jew stood before me, waiting.

"You want to sleep all tied up like an animal?" he exclaimed sourly. Getting behind me he began sawing away at the rope that bound my hands together. The small of my back contracted painfully, in expectation of the sharp, penetrating dig of the knife. I stood stiff, saying more prayers in that moment than ever before in my life. But nothing happened to me; the ropes fell from my hands, and he motioned me to the table on which he had placed a large piece of black bread and several slices of meat. So I saw I was not to be slaughtered at present.

I tasted the bread and meat rather gingerly, as if it might be poisoned, but my hunger grew as I ate, and I soon devoured it in big mouthfuls. The old man had brought a horn, and was pouring brown beer from it into a mug.

When I had eaten and drunk I got up; I saw that the Jew was watching me stealthily, and I stood smoothing my hair in embarrassment.

"You are vain that you are handsome?" he asked. His voice was as if split into two thin threads; he said each word separately, as if he did not know the language well.

I suppose I blushed. I had no idea how to talk to the old Jew. How could one talk respectfully to a Jew? Yet—he was my master. An odd master, after the splendid lord of the castle! I pictured how my lord would have looked at this old Jew—with what proud disgust, what contempt—and how the boys would mock me if they knew.

I stared down at the floor, silent as a creature of wood. The Jew took up the taper from the table and beckoned me to follow him. I slunk after him up another flight of steps, narrower than the first, and came to an attic. Under the sharply sloped roof the full moon looked gently through a square hole which served as a window; the sight of it comforted me a little, reminding me of the lovely nights in the fields, when I still lived at my mother's hut. The thought of my mother then came so strongly over me that my eyes blurred; I scarcely saw the low pallet which the weird little stooping figure, like an actual sorcerer, pointed out to me, while the shadows danced behind the candle. I flung myself down on the bed, and as soon as I heard the old man's light, faltering steps growing fainter down the stairs I began to gasp and weep, and finally to sob out loud.

Several times during that long, dreadful night I woke up quaking with horror and loneliness; the outline of a rooftop across the road looked to me like a giant's boot and I pic-

tured a huge body spread out over the streets. The howling of a cat gave me such a thrill of fear that I was half up before I understood what the sound really was. Being up, I suddenly planned to escape and even stole out of the bed and began to creep down the cold, black stairway. But my senses came back to me; I realized that even if I could get to the street door without being overheard, how could I force the locks and unbar the large beam, not to mention drawing the rusted bolts, the noise of which would have awakened the whole house? I saw that I was compelled to wait until daytime. I crept back and, lying down, determined to force myself to sleep. But I must have been more tired than I thought, for sleep came at once, and I was surprised to open my eyes on a window quite blue with early morning light.

A tiny boy, still in his night clothes, was standing beside me. His large brown eyes were lively with interest, his tangled black curls stood up comically around his head, and his toes peeped out from under his garment.

"Bad boy. Wake up now," he remarked solemnly.

As I lay sleepily staring at him, the little apparition disappeared. An old woman's voice was heard in hushed scolding. I must have fallen asleep at once, for I woke again restless under the sun's beams, which were pouring straight into my eyes. I hastily dressed, and ran down the steps.

I came upon my master standing in the room which I had entered the night before. His face was turned to the wall, and he was muttering strangely to himself, for all the world like a wizard. He turned his head, noticed me, and still muttering, motioned me to a door, from which steps led down into a courtyard. I let myself out and made my way to a pump. Near the pump I found a pail, with some rain water in the bottom; I crossed myself, poured out the water, refilled it from the pump, and washed.

A dragging, shuffling sound behind me made me turn with a start; it was an old woman coming through the yard, across the bumpy cobblestones. She carried a large empty pail which she motioned me to fill. As I drew the water, I felt her little eyes fixed cunningly on me, under her brown, wrinkled forehead; no hair was visible, her head being tightly wrapped in a black kerchief. I followed her back to the house, and up a different flight of stairs. She made me set down the water outside a tall door. As I turned to go down again, the door opened halfway, and a girl's head looked out and withdrew quickly.

My master's name was Pesach ben Leib; I saw the whole family—himself, his grandson, and his granddaughter—at the dinner table at noon. I had passed the morning at the orders of Miriam, the old serving-woman; she made me chop wood, sweep the yard, blow the bellows for the fire in the large room, and carry her basket to and from the market. I was bewildered and sickened, as I walked through the streets with her, by the sight of such crowds of Jews in their horned hats and long gaberdines with the yellow badges. And their language was such a mixture of Bohemian and some other tongue that I hardly understood it.

I tried to tell the old woman that I knew how to help in the cooking, but as soon as she caught my meaning, she thrust me away with a look of horror, as if I intended to poison the food. I found out afterward that it was because the Jews have a thousand rules and restrictions in regard to preparing food, and the mere touch of a Gentile would be enough to make them throw the meal out.

When dinnertime came, I did not know what to do, nor where I would be permitted to eat, for there was no sign of a table being set in the kitchen for the servants. My master came into the large room first, and sat down at the head of the table, from which the little wooden figures which I had seen there the night before had been removed. Next I saw the old serving-woman leading by the hand the little brown-eyed boy, or rather, being led by him, for he tugged and pulled her along. An old manservant, the husband of the woman, now hobbled in. To my amazement, they sat down at the master's table.

I stood by the wall, looking at the bowl of hot soup, and wondering what to do. Reb Pesach sat waiting, with a small black cap on his head.

"What is your name?" he asked.

"Tomás," I said, glad to be remembered before the meal began.

"Wash your hands and sit down," he said, nodding to one of the two empty seats which remained.

I went out, dipped my hands in the water pail in the yard, dried them, and came back, blushing at the thought of having to eat with Jews; but I was afraid to make any objection. I crossed myself as I sat down; I saw the old man wince, but he said nothing.

Still we waited. Soon the door opened quietly, and the girl whose head I had seen peering out of the doorway upstairs came in. She was pale and pretty in a quiet way; her fair hair was braided; her eyes were gray and had a still look, but I thought they opened a little wider as she glanced at me. She sat all through the meal without turning her silent head, although two faint lines of troubled thought formed between her brows.

Whenever it was necessary to bring anything to the table, the serving-woman got up and carried it in, but most of the meal had been placed there at the start. After saying prayers, in which even the little boy pretended to join, we began to eat. The food had a strange taste, at first, and the embarrassment

and bewilderment which I felt made it almost stick in my throat, but I was healthily hungry, and the food was fresh and plentiful, so I fancy I ate my full share.

The days passed; there were hundreds of odd jobs to be done, and I did them. While marketing or drawing water at the well in the central market place I found myself making acquaintances, after all; the young Jewish boys did not seem so different from those I had known, except for their dark complexions and nervous, clever look. I saw them fighting each other and helping each other, just as naturally as we used to do at the castle. They were a little strange with me at first, as I was with them, but when I upset a basketful of turnips and cabbages they all came running to help me pick them up before they should be scattered. One small fellow even came hurrying after me, when they were all gathered, with a little turnip which had rolled into a hole and for a while had escaped being found. I couldn't help smiling as I took it, and instantly a roar of laughter broke from the other boys. After that I often stopped and played games with them, although old Miriam scolded me when I returned late.

I did not see much of Mademoiselle Rachel, the granddaughter; she kept to her room a great deal, sewing, embroidering, or weaving. She made ornamental covers for the bread and for the tables, but mostly she made things for herself. Her father, who was dead, had been a pearl setter and she had many pretty pearl ornaments and loose pearls, which she used in various ways. Once she sewed some on the front of a festival dress; at another time she made a little cap and fastened small pearls all over it—it was pretty. She was very quiet, but sometimes when I caught a glimpse of her sitting idle over her work, or looking out of her half-open window with a curious waiting expression, I wondered if she had some trouble that occupied her mind.

One day she surprised me by calling me abruptly into her room.

"You said your name is Tomás?" Her cheek was flushed and she spoke in a hurried, nervous tone, glancing at the door, which she had purposely left open.

"Yes, ma'amselle," I replied.

"I thought you—you looked a little like—But you—do you know him?—Lucien?"

"Lucien!" I exclaimed. "Monsieur Lucien—my lord's page?"

"Yes, yes, his page," she agreed, and her eyes were wonderfully bright for a moment. "He—" She stopped, then she looked up at me defiantly.

"You—you do not know when my lord will come again?" she ventured, then ran on quickly: "You see, he has borrowed so much money from my grandfather; we—I thought—he would have returned some of it—by this time." She seemed to be waiting for a reply, but I could not think of anything to say.

"You may go, thank you . . . Don't tell my grandfather that—that I spoke to you; he does not think it nice for me to speak to anyone but Miriam and the baby." She moved away with a little toss of her head, and I went downstairs.

By this time I was feeling at home in the house, and even in the Ghetto. The strangeness of the houses, their closeness, the narrow street, the crowds of children became more and more natural to my eyes. For a long time I regretted my companions at the castle and the pride of serving there, but I was quite willing to do without the frequent scoldings and whippings of the cooks and footmen, the haughtiness of the pages, the fear of my lord, and the noise and heat of the kitchens.

Joseph, the little boy, took a liking to me; he used to follow me all over the house and the yard with his doll and some shapeless wooden things which he played with. Sometimes he would clasp his arm around my knee, bruising my skin with the "toys" which he held fast in his fists, and would insist on walking with me when I went to the market; he was usually too proud to permit himself to be carried, though that would have been much easier for both of us. And what a howl he would set up when old Miriam would not let him sweep the floor with the besom five times his height! He was an early riser, I found out; more than once I had a terrible dream that I was hanging on the side of a house and the crows were pecking out my eyes, only to wake and find little Joseph standing beside me, trying to pluck my eyelids open with his fingers.

There was not much scolding or crossness in that house or indeed in all the Ghetto, as far as I could observe. The people talked loud and fast, with much excitement but very little anger. I never saw a child or a woman being beaten, and the servants were always kindly treated. I received a new suit of clothes to wear on the Jewish Sabbath, and was not allowed to do any work that day besides lighting the fires. When I fell ill the whole house was kept in a hush; food was brought up to me, medicines were prepared and given me; Mademoiselle Rachel herself made soup for me, and it was good, too.

It was so different from the castle, where one servant or one peasant more or less didn't matter, and where there was always the question whether the value of a serf was equal to the cost of curing him.

But I was certainly less free here than at the castle. As for my mother, it was quite impossible to steal away to see her, for the Ghetto gates were guarded day and night. My own good meals would hardly go down my throat, when I thought how she and my little sister and brothers must be starving.

I stood one evening by the fire in the large room, alone except for the master, who was sitting by the table with his inkhorn and quill, writing on parchment in those queer letters which at that time still seemed to me to be enchanted symbols. Suddenly the longing for my mother came up like a ball of fire in my throat; the tears stole out of my eyes and ran down my cheeks. My master, looking up at that moment, frowned, and his cheeks grew faintly red above his gray beard.

"What is the matter? You are not happy? Perhaps I beat you? Perhaps you do not eat good food?" he inquired crossly.

I did not answer, for fear that my voice would sound as if I were crying.

"Well, why do you weep?" he exclaimed.

I stammered out something about my mother's sickness. Pesach ben Leib frowned more angrily than ever.

"You are a fine son!" he stormed. "For so long you are here, and who knows even if you have not—God forbid—a mother? You sleep and you eat and you never think of her. A mother—I suppose one picks up a mother in every corner, ha?" His big horn spectacles were dragging off his nose; he went out of the room twirling his earlocks and mumbling angrily.

I was very indignant at the undeserved scolding, but hopeful, nevertheless. When my master returned, old Meir, the manservant, was following sleepily at his heels, fumbling with the strings of his jacket, which his nervous old fingers found it hard to tie. He had evidently been waked up. Behind him marched old Miriam, carrying a large covered basket; she darted a malicious little smile at me as I took it from her.

"Meir, you shall take him to the gate of the Ghetto. Come, Tomás, you naughty fellow, you must go; do not be lazy, but hurry." He followed me, driving me all the way to the outside door, as if I were an unwilling schoolboy. My heart was so full that I took his brown-spotted hand with the soft wrinkled veins standing up under the skin, and kissed it, as Meir and I went out the door.

At the gate of the Ghetto, Meir left me and went back. I had to bang on the door, wake the watchman, and explain to him that I was not a Jew before he would let me out. I ran straight up across the bridge, wild with freedom, hurrying till my breath came short and the basket knocked against my side; then I saw it would be better to go slowly and not exhaust myself. If only my mother were still there to receive the basket! I said I don't know how many aves and paternosters as I ran over the cobbles that were deep in mud.

I soon came out to the fields and drew in the fresh, free air in long, deep breaths; it seemed I could not fill my lungs quickly enough with its clean strength. I ran toward the uneven line of the hut roofs, drawn in black against the sky. It seemed my feet would never get me there. When I reached our door, I stopped outside awhile, scarcely daring to enter. It was opened from within by my little brother Klaus, who must have heard my steps.

The whole family jumped at me with delight. Klaus immediately began complaining that there was no bread and he was hungry. But my father held my hand tight and brought me over to my mother, who was lying on a heap of straw, smiling faintly at me in the light of a burning rag that floated in a dish of grease.

She whispered to the children to hush, while I told them what had happened to me. When she heard that I was now the servant of a Jew she clasped her hands in pain and looked up, her lips moving, to the little statue of the Virgin on the wall. I drooped my head in shame, so she caressed me, and put up her frail hand to pat my cheeks; she smiled and said, "You are not thin, dear; you have enough to eat."

A shout from behind told me that the children had already investigated the basket; they were dancing about, with pieces of bread, chicken, and cake in their hands and mouths. I snatched the basket before they could quite empty it; Mother sat up, her eyes shining, and distributed the best parts, until I made her stop or she would have left nothing for herself. And my father, munching away with a look of happy contentment on his hollow cheeks, said, "Your master will certainly become a Christian; have you been converting him, Tomás?"

I would have been ashamed to tell my old

companions, when I saw them in the morning, that I served a Jew, but my little brothers saved me the trouble by telling everything to the neighbors before I woke up. The older people looked somber and shook their heads, and told my father and mother that evil would certainly come of these devilish tricks and that perhaps spells had been laid on the food sent them and they would be possessed by demons. So Mother sent for the priest; he blessed us and she felt safe again, but I did not think it was really necessary. It was with a heavy heart that I left the fresh-smelling fields to go back to the gloom of the Ghetto.

When I came outside the gates of the Jewish quarter I saw a group of children playing; they were throwing small stones at some empty flasks which they had made to stand up in a row against the wall. I laughed at their bad shots, but did not laugh so loud when a stray pebble hit me. But the little fellow who had thrown it stood looking bashfully at me with his dirty finger in his rosy mouth, so I passed in without scolding him.

It was still quite early in the morning, and most of the men were in the synagogue at their prayers. I walked briskly along, enjoying the freshness of the unbreathed air, while the cool, silvery light of the sky warmed into golden as the sun reached the tops of the houses.

Coming out from one of the winding turns of the road where our house was, I was just crossing to my master's doorway when I noticed a figure leaning against the wall looking toward Mademoiselle Rachel's window. It was a young man, a gentleman, judging by his sword and the clothes of velvet which I saw under his coarse cloak. Something about the form and pose of the man gave me a thrill of fear and familiarity. Yes, it *was* my lord! I jumped back, all trembling, into a deep doorway and looked out cautiously.

At the window Mademoiselle Rachel's head had appeared; her cheeks were lightly flushed, and she shook her fair braids with a reluctant but obstinate motion. My lord turned his head and looked up with his saucy, charming smile, as if much amused by her resistance; then he stretched out his arms as if inviting her to jump down and let him carry her away. But at that she moved back with a startled motion. My lord frowned imploringly; she put her hand up to her eyes, then she quickly drew back and closed the shutters.

My lord's face changed in an instant; he sent dark looks of anger through his narrowed eyes at the fast-shut window, and hurried off, his nostrils inflating spitefully. I followed him at a good distance. He came to the Ghetto gate, elbowing out of his way everyone who passed within reach of him; I forgot to say that he had put on his mask when he left our house. He stopped outside the gate, as if to take breath, and he needed to, for he had gone at such a rate that I had hardly kept up with him.

The children were still there, but they were not playing. They were clustered together, looking up fearfully at a priest, who was talking quickly and shaking a crucifix in their faces. Two of the smallest boys were still throwing stones at the bottles. As I looked, one of the stones went astray and struck the priest a sharp blow on the lip. The terrified children began to run back to the gates. His face wrinkling and red with fury, the priest dashed after them, holding one hand to his bleeding lip. But my lord, lifting his hand to attract the priest's attention, smiled with eager malice.

"The vile Jews have been insulting the crucifix!" he exclaimed. "They have thrown stones at the sacred image! As a servant of God, sir priest, I call upon you to resent it. I would rouse the people of the town, and if you went to the castle there would probably be soldiers there ready to defend the cause of their Lord and Saviour."

The priest hesitated; he looked quiveringly at my lord, struggling to decide whether to take immediate satisfaction upon the children, or to have a richer revenge by setting the mob upon the whole Ghetto. Just then one of the vanishing children, thinking himself safe, put up his hand to his nose in a gesture of contempt. The priest turned purple and dashed after him.

But my lord caught hold of the priest's robe.

"Wait," he commanded. "See here, good friend and holy sir, I am a witness to a shameful crime which has been committed against our holy religion." And he took off his mask. The priest's surprise made him sag down like a bag of flour whose string has been untied, and his eyes opened, round and glassy and hard, like grapes. My lord drew him further away from the gate. I could not hear their words any more; I only saw the priest's head bobbing up and down, while my lord patted him familiarly on the back. So they walked off, until two horses came slowly trotting toward them; one carried Monsieur Lucien, the other was without a rider. Lucien jumped down and held my lord's stirrup; as they trotted away I heard their laughter in a united burst.

That same day I received the only beating I ever had among the Jews. It was not a real beating either. I was so wrapped up in thoughts as to what Mademoiselle Rachel was doing and what my lord and the priest were planning that I dropped several rolls of manuscript which my master had ordered me to bring him; they unrolled all the way down the stairs, and there was a fine muddle. Now, my master, who was very wealthy, spent comparatively little on his household, but he put fortunes into buying old Hebrew books and manuscripts. Something had evidently been making him irritable, for when he saw the dropped parchments, which kept unrolling as if with deliberate obstinacy, his wrath boiled over; he strode up to me and gave me a box on each ear that made me sit down on the floor very hard.

I was more surprised at his rage and at the unexpected strength of his arm than hurt by the blows. I picked myself up rather dazed; to tell the truth, my ears were ringing. But a still greater surprise was to come. Mademoiselle Rachel had seen the blows; she came rushing up to me, felt my ears as if to see whether they were still on, and turning to her grandfather, she gave him a hearty rating for mistreating the "stranger within his gates," as she put it. Her quiet face was flaming, and her gray eyes seemed to have sparks in them. I honestly wondered what all the fuss was about, but the old man came up to me very kindly and asked my pardon for having struck me. Then he sharply ordered Mademoiselle Rachel to go to her room, and she went with her head in the air.

I recalled then that as I came back into the house I had heard the two of them talking upstairs rather angrily. I heard my master say, "*I* am forced to deal with him, but for *you* there is no occasion!" Then Mademoiselle Rachel answered something I couldn't distinguish, but she sounded quite offended, and then a door slammed shut. So I supposed it was a quarrel about my lord talking to her outside her window that had upset them both.

Time passed, peaceably enough for others, but for me there was no rest. I knew my lord too well by this time to think that he would let anything he really wanted escape his grasp. I understood the matter now; he had evidently been attracted to Mademoiselle Rachel. He would get her into his power in some way. What he was planning to do? And the priest—what was his share in it?

At last I heard news that relieved me a little. I had gone to see my family—my master let me go every week, unless there was something important to be done—and there the boys told me that they had heard from the servants of some gentleman of the Emperor's court, who was visiting the castle, that the Emperor, being in need of money, was planning to enter into a compact with certain prominent and wealthy Jews, promising their people royal protection from attacks in return for a considerable sum of money to be paid into the royal treasury. So I stopped worrying and let the matter go out of my mind.

It was summer, and the damp walls of the Ghetto houses steamed in the sun. It was no warmer within the houses, however, especially in the wine cellars. The inside of these Jewish houses wound about and in and out like the inner part of a sponge. In our house there were one or two secret doors opening onto a staircase cut in the thickness of the wall, twisting and turning in black darkness to lead at last into the cellar of a house on the next street. Old Meir told me that this staircase had been built for escape in case of attack.

"That won't be needed now," I said confidently and told him the news from court.

He made a grimace at me, hitching up one side of his faded, whiskered face.

"Agreements!" he mumbled. "The master knows all about it. Go and talk to him."

The master had indeed heard of the com-

pact, and was quite cheerful over it. He patted me on the back and began walking up and down the room before the fire, his hand up to his mouth, smiling and glancing at me shrewdly now and then.

"Tomás," he said at last, "tomorrow is Sabbath. You will go with me to the synagogue for once." I must have looked scared, for he added, frowning, "To accompany Joseph, who goes for the first time."

So the next morning—it was a pleasant day, a little cloudy, but with a warm wind blowing from the fields—I followed my master and Mademoiselle Rachel to the synagogue. Joseph trotted along beside me, holding my hand and chewing his thumb. I carried a little box in which was a small silk prayer shawl for the child. The synagogue is opposite the Jewish town hall; a little round, age-blackened building it is, with a stepped gable that gives it a sawlike silhouette. There are two or three high, narrow windows of oblong shape, and one round one in which is set the sign of the shield of David. It is an insignificant place, compared with the noble Gothic towers and arches of the cathedrals

of Prague. The Ghetto town hall is a finer building; it has two clocks, one of which has Hebrew letters instead of numerals, and hands that go backwards. But the clock on our great Tyn Cathedral is much more interesting, I think. There are two little doors in the tower, right over the clock face, and every time the clock strikes, these doors open and the figures of the twelve apostles come out and move about in the doorways.

Mademoiselle Rachel left us at the entrance to go around to the women's side of the synagogue. I gave Joseph his shawl, and told him to follow his grandfather, but he clutched my hand and said, "Doseph f'ightened." His lower lip pushed slowly out and his eyelids dropped in a way that I recognized as the introduction to a howl. So I said an Ave Maria and prayed for forgiveness and went in with him.

I could see why he was frightened, poor little fellow! There were hundreds of men, it seemed, old and young, bearded and with earlocks, wrapped in their prayer shawls, bending about and glancing everywhere with a faraway look in their eyes, muttering and

shouting and weeping and chanting. Hardly any sunlight struggled in; one could only see a muddle of shawled heads, twisted iron chandeliers, worm-eaten reading desks, and black crisscross shadows.

There was no order, no decorum. People walked in at all times; everyone prayed as he pleased, interrupting himself to nod to a friend or to ask after the family, strolling about among those earnestly praying. The confusion seemed to go on interminably, until at last nearly everybody stopped praying, backs were straightened, prayer shawls were folded, kissed, and tucked away somewhere in the seats, a murmur of conversation arose, and soon they were all talking and telling jokes and arguing.

And what did they not discuss! There were disputations going on at the time, by order of the Pope, between many famous Jewish rabbis and some Catholic dignitaries of our Holy Church; the Jews went over all the proceedings to date, expressed their opinions of the arguments used on both sides, told how *they* would have answered if they were taking part in the dispute, and expressed praise or

regret. They talked of business, of chess, (those little wooden figures which I had seen on the table the first day I came were only chessmen, not puppets), of weather for sailing ships, of money prices and rates of interest; of the new maps being made by the Mallorcan Jews, of a wonderful cure achieved by the Jewish physician of the Duke of Savoy, of the famous Jewish pirate who was preparing to meet an attack of the Spanish galleys; of trouble with the trade guilds in Italy; of new methods of manufacturing copper and preparing it for commerce—a worldful of matters! Then came blessings, and "God be with you's" and "Length of days unto you's" —in Hebrew, which my master translated to Joseph and to me.

It seemed long enough before we reached home, and I had an excellent appetite for the good soup and chicken and white bread. Joseph babbled all through the meal, his mouth full, telling us of the wonders of the synagogue, and of the tall man who had patted him on the head and the dog that had licked his hand in the street.

After dinner he made me take him on my

shoulder and carry him about the streets—
he had hardly ever been out of our street
before, except to the market, which was near
by—and he held on to me with one hand in
my hair, which had grown to its former
length, while he chattered and pointed with
his finger at all the strange sights he encoun-
tered.

Outside an inn, I observed several boys
imitating my master; they copied his walk
and talked to each other in his stilted sarcastic
way, and shrieked with laughter. When they
saw me they grabbed Joseph off my shoulder
and played with him, chasing him and teas-
ing him until he squealed. So I lifted him
onto my shoulder again, in spite of the boys'
protests, and brought him home, for I thought
he had had enough excitement.

I remember this Saturday—I shall remember it all my life. It was the last I spent in
the household of Pesach ben Leib.

On the next Sabbath the blow fell, and
this was the manner of it.

The disputations, which had been held
mainly for the purpose of converting the Jews
by reason, had been by no means a sure vic-

tory for the upholders of Christ. In fact, it was said openly in the Ghetto that the victory properly belonged to the Jews. The Pope tartly declared that no Christian might henceforth argue with Jews, unless he felt that his faith was strong enough to withstand all reason. It was also decided by the Church that the superior arguments of the Jews were due to the fact that they were cunning of mind; the true answers existed, only the Church priests had not happened to think of them. Now, with all reverence to Holy Church, I did not think this was reasonable; but then I was only an ignorant serf, and what did I know of the ways of the great and holy?

A new matter—or rather, an old one renewed—was also inciting the people against the Jews: a certain writer—I forget his name —had been declaring that the Talmud, as the Jews call their book, was full of wickedness; that it ordered Jews to kill Christian children and to drink their blood at the Passover; that it taught them it was unlawful to save a Christian's life, or to help him; that the Jews insulted the sacred Host and had dealings with the Devil. I know that once I

had believed all this myself, but I c
told them now it was not true. I
how my master lent a large sum
without security, to a penniless noble.
pay a fine to the Emperor in lieu of losing his
life; and it was never returned. But people
did not seem to care about these things; my
own family, whom I went to see the following
Friday, listened doubtfully to what I told
them about the truth of these matters.

My master had told me what the prayers at
the festivals meant; I had even picked up a
few words of Hebrew, though against my
will. But I saw that the difference between
the laws of the Jews and those of Christ is not
as great as people imagine. Certainly they are
kind to each other, and to their servants, and
to strangers, Christian or Jewish. They are
good, too, in their home life.

Well, my misfortune was that I had gone
to see my family on Friday and had stayed
overnight. In the morning Klaus wanted me
to help him do his share of the work in the
fields; he said he was not feeling very strong.
I should have told the lazy fellow to attend to
his own work without asking help, but you

see, I felt a little apologetic, because I had good food and kind treatment all the time, and he was ill-fed and was often beaten by the bailiff's men.

I forgot to say that Mother was worried about my soul, and made me wear my crucifix night and day, and made me promise to say my prayers; but she need not have worried. Many Christian servants, I know, did give up their faith, but that was because they knew that if they were converted to Judaism they would never have to serve Christian masters again; but I would not be mean enough to do it for such a reason.

Well, I was saying that I stayed to help my brother, and afterwards, being in a hurry to reach my master's home, I cut across the sown fields and came to the Ghetto gates. Across the bridge a multitude of people were pouring, both ways at once, struggling and shrieking, mad with rage and fear. From the dismal roofs of the Ghetto black smoke was coming up in brief surges, as if pumped from below; sometimes the puffs were alive with a vicious red flame. The fire seemed to pant with red breath upon the pleasant sky, and the innocent, light clouds floated, now silvery and pearl-pale, now an angry dark pink as if dissolved in blood.

And below! My eyes refused to see for a minute, while someone seemed to have taken hold of my head and spun it around and around till I was ready to fall. But no one had touched me; I was leaning, faint and sick, my hands trembling like paper, against the low wall of the bridge. The mob pushed and jostled within a foot of me; I saw knives being plunged into Jewish breasts and thighs; I saw daggers being torn, crimson-wet, out of living throats.

I came to life. I pushed and strove like a madman, driving my elbows and lowered head into everything that stood in my way; I ran over dead bodies; I stepped on fallen and wounded people. Someone shouted my name, a hand seized me by the wrist—I don't know who it was; I beat him off, and got past the crashed-in gates into the Ghetto.

The streets were full of smoke that blinded me and stung my eyes until I could hardly make my way about. I stumbled often, and always over dead bodies—women, one of the boys who had played with Joseph last Sabbath —children, too. I found myself crying aloud like a child as I ran, yet I scarcely realized that I was weeping. Near our street, a pitiful barricade of a few wooden beams had been put up and broken down; and bodies hung, crumpled like rags, in the charred ruins of the houses.

The smoke had thinned to a bluish mist in our street; I dashed to our door. It was broken open. I called; my voice echoed; there was no answer. I clung to the doorpost; my breath would not come; I thought I was suffocating. I slipped inside the door and dropped alongside the steps. I had noticed that the gables of our house were beginning to smolder from a burning beam that had fallen from the roof of the next house, which was higher than ours; but I thought I did not care whether I was burned inside the doorway or not. My heart felt sick with anguish.

It seemed only a minute till I heard sounds outside—the neighing of a startled horse, the breathless, gay voice of my lord.

"Here, Lucien! Do you see? There's her window. Run up and bring her to the—no, bring her down; you will have time . . ."

"Perhaps she has gone away, my lord? The door is broken open."

"Ah, *peste!* Go and see!"

A nimble, slender figure appeared, darted up the steps, and vanished upstairs. I actually smiled to myself, as I lay dizzy and silly on the threshold. Had I not seen a torn veil caught on the latch, and some scraps of scribbled parchment on the floor? Mademoiselle Rachel, the master, the boy—no more than a baby—they were gone. I dragged myself to my feet to get away, for the presence of my lord, gaily sitting on his horse outside, was too much for me to bear.

As I got up I heard a cry from my lord; a gale of bitter black smoke drove down the stairway into the street.

"Lucien! Lucien! The whole place is on fire! Let the Jewish brat burn, confound her! Come out!"

I ran, half-choked, into the street; through thick smoke I discerned the figure of my lord on his frightened horse, gigantic and overclouded. The steed reared back, neighing; my lord cursed, struggling to rein it in, and beating its head with his whip. When he saw my figure through the smoke, he cried:

"Ah, Lucien! . . . Follow me to the gates . . . I can't hold this miserable animal . . ." He gave the horse its head and it dashed madly off, banging itself heedlessly against the jutting-out houses, till it vanished around the corner.

So he had taken me for Lucien! In the crazy fit that possessed me I wanted to laugh and laugh. He had gone off, and that precious page of his was burning to death in the blazing house! It served him right! It served him right! It was Christ's punishment on them both!

A loud scream from above brought me to my cold senses. At Mademoiselle Rachel's lattice, Monsieur Lucien was standing, surrounded by flames as a portrait by its frame. His face was gray and quivering, his hands were stretched shaking out of the window. He must have been stupefied with terror, for he never attempted to turn back and go down; he just stood there, stretching out his hands and uttering shriek after shriek.

No, I could not bear it; nobody could have borne it. I think my lord himself could not have seen a Jew in such terror without trying to save him. Hating them both as I did, I ran back into the doorway and up the smoking steps. A fearful burst of heat, like a wind from hell, enveloped me; everything was faint as a dream for a moment. I worked my way up those cursed, twisting steps, my heart banging slow and heavy in my breast, till I imagined it was a leaden hammer which I had to keep on lifting and dropping, lifting and dropping.

I got to Mademoiselle Rachel's room. That door, too, was broken in . . . her pearled cap lay on the floor . . . I almost turned back.

I came to Monsieur Lucien through the fire and put my arms around him; he was half in a faint. He seized me around the neck and fell in a heavy mass against me.

I carried him to the secret doorway and dragged him out onto the dark stone staircase, horribly damp and cold after the blazing house. He lay with his head slumped on my shoulder; the cold air and the damp brought him to consciousness. Suddenly he seemed to have a realization of what was happening; he tried to stand up, looking at me with a kind of horror. But I said through set teeth, "Shut your mouth and hold on to me!" for he could have broken my neck by causing me to make a misstep on those narrow, erratic stairs.

When we emerged into the other street, the smoke had cleared; the burned houses still smoldered, with small blue flames lingering in the charred joists and corner beams. One could almost smell the air again. The street was empty save for the inevitable crushed and burned bodies.

Monsieur Lucien was a gentleman; he came of the best blood in France. As soon as I let him go he braced himself, rocking a little on his feet, wetting his lips with his tongue—and smiled. It was a pitiful, wavering smile to be on those haughty lips. It vanished in a moment and unconquerable tears suddenly made his eyes large and glittering.

"I—I—believe me, Tomás, I wouldn't have —lost—my head—like that— It was not so much the fire, but—he—he left me there, to burn, like a J—" He stopped. "When I looked into the street, and I—saw his horse going around—the—corner—" He gave up; he leaned his face against the wall, with his hands up to his cheeks, and sobbed.

The words were forced out of my mouth. I don't know why I said them. I should have let him suffer—and let my lord try afterwards to clear himself of the charge of cowardly neglect of his page.

"Monsieur Lucien," I began, "he didn't leave you here to burn . . . He saw me in the smoke . . ."

Lucien turned upon me, his face slowly freeing itself of heartbreak, his eyes growing larger and lighter.

"He—we—the resemblance!" he exclaimed.

"He thought it was you . . . And now go to the depths of hell away from here!" I cried, suddenly faint with rage.

Monsieur Lucien remained looking at me, and for once there was real remorse in his face. He made a step forward and offered me his hand, but I could not take it. He stood shamefaced, murmuring, "My lord will be waiting for me," and started off, then turned and flew back again, seized me in his arms, kissed me on both cheeks, exclaimed, "I will remember!" and hurried down the street. He

looked back before he reached the corner, then disappeared.

I could not keep still; I wandered about through the empty houses, in and out of doorways, up and down streets, thinking nothing and feeling nothing, for there was a gripping clutch on my heart that hurt too much to let me feel anything more . . . I fell asleep somewhere—I think it was on a gravestone in the old cemetery . . .

It was three days before I learned what had actually happened. The raging beasts of the mob had made a human bonfire. They had dragged the Jews out of their houses, men, women, and children, and brought them down to the market place. Scores of bodies were found in a heap, outside a mass of ruined houses. When I went there the wind was blowing the black flakes and fragments here and there. I searched, my eyes blind with bitterness, my hand trembling so that I could hardly pick up what I found. After a long while I found a scrap of molten silver with a pearl in it—some girl's ornament—and a tiny, blackened pearl ring near by . . .

Yet often I remind myself—when the sharp

sorrow of it pierces through my sleep till I wake up—that there were families who were saved from the slaughter, that Jews were found wandering miles from town, living in the woods, or harbored on the humble farms of Christian people who felt the black shame of what had been done. I am a clerk at the monastery now, placed here through the help of Monsieur Lucien, but I shall yet some day make search for those whom I loved—yes, loved, Jews though they were. And who knows? Perhaps some day I shall find them again, little Joseph, and my gentle maiden, Mademoiselle Rachel, and the old man who taught me from his Hebrew soul the loving-kindness which I had never known. I shall find them, and I shall help them and work for them with my two strong hands, and among us we shall learn that the God of mercy is the same God, no matter where we find Him.

Sulamith Ish-Kishor was born in London, England, where she spent the early years of her life. She began to write at the age of five, and when she was ten years old a number of her poems were published. After her arrival with her family in the United States she attended Wadleigh High School and Hunter College, where she specialized in history, English, and foreign languages. A prolific writer, Miss Ish-Kishor has contributed articles to numerous magazines, and among the books she has written are *Children's History of Israel* and *American Promise*.

Ben Shahn, one of America's foremost artists, was born in Kovno, Russia, in 1898 and came to the United States in 1906. Upon the completion of his studies at the National Academy of Design and New York University, he worked as a photographer and designer and then taught art at such institutions as the University of Colorado, Black Mountain College, Brooklyn Museum, and Harvard University. His works are part of many important private and museum collections throughout the world. Well known also for his graphic work, he has illustrated several books, among which are *A Partridge in a Pear Tree*, and *Kay-Kay Comes Home*.